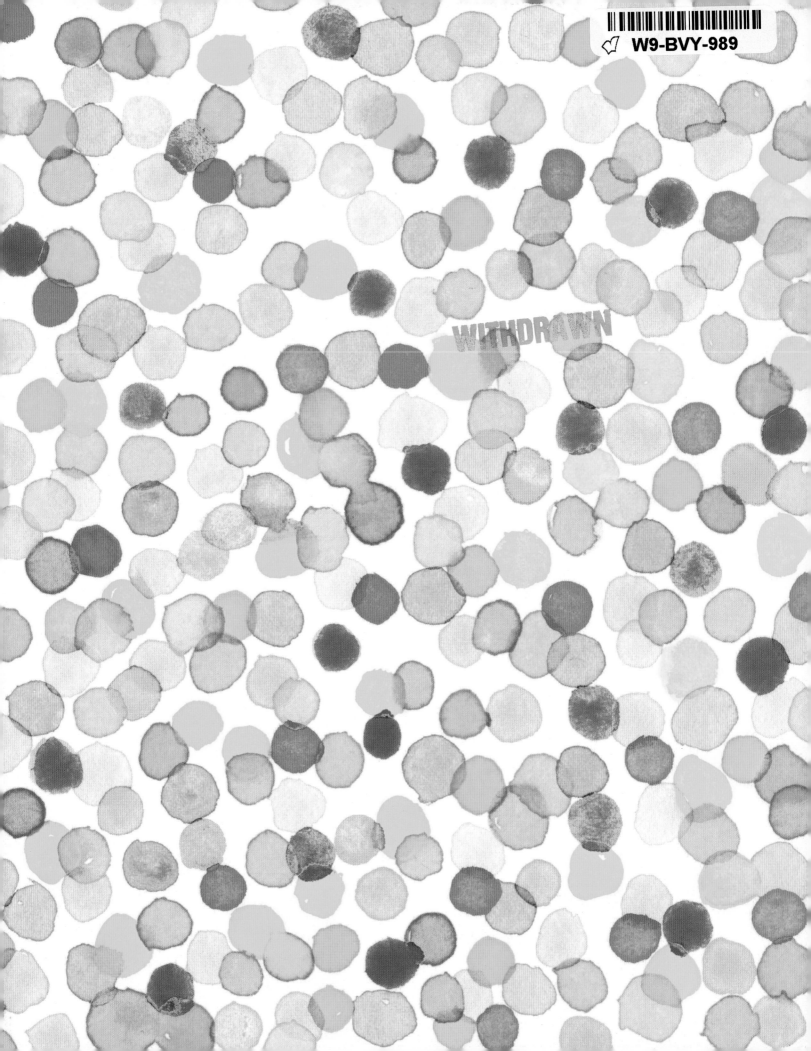

To Félicien and all little budding designers

All rights reserved. Published in the United States by Random House Studio, an imprint of Random House Children's Books,
a division of Penguin Random House LLC, New York.

Random House Studio with colophon is a trademark of Penguin Random House LLC.

Visit us on the Web! rhcbooks.com
Educators and librarians, for a variety of teaching tools, visit us at RHTeachersLibrarians.com

Library of Congress Cataloging-in-Publication Data
Name: Kerascoët, author, illustrator. • Title: I forgive Alex : a simple story about understanding / Kerascoët.
Description: First edition. | New York : Random House Studio, [2022] | Audience: Ages 4–8. | Summary: When an energetic child inadvertently
upsets one of his classmates, everyone is reminded that it is important to take responsibility for a mistake,
and it is equally important to be ready to forgive. Includes information about apologies and forgiveness.
Identifiers: LCCN 2021042522 (print) | LCCN 2021042523 (ebook) | ISBN 978-0-593-38150-2 (trade) | ISBN 978-0-593-38151-9 (lib. bdg.)
ISBN 978-0-593-38152-6 (ebook)
Subjects: CYAC: Stories without words. | Interpersonal relations—Fiction.
Forgiveness—Fiction. | LCGFT: Picture books. | Wordless picture books.
Classification: LCC PZ7.1.K5093 Iaf 2018 (print) | LCC PZ7.1.K5093 (ebook) | DDC [E]—dc23

The illustrations were rendered in ink and watercolor.

MANUFACTURED IN CHINA
10 9 8 7 6 5 4 3 2 1
First Edition

Drawing on last page of story by Rosalie Cosset (age 9).

The authors would like to thank Jinnie Spiegler, Director of Curriculum and Training at the Anti-Defamation
League (ADL), for her help with the information about apologies and forgiveness on the last page.

I FORGIVE ALEX

A SIMPLE STORY ABOUT UNDERSTANDING

by Kerascoët

RANDOM HOUSE STUDIO
NEW YORK

FOR CHILDREN
WHAT TO DO WHEN YOU HURT SOMEONE:
You can hurt someone's feelings or make them angry, even if you don't mean to. If that happens, here are some things to keep in mind:

- Relationships are important. When there is conflict, it's good to talk about it so the relationship can improve and grow.

- Think about how your actions impact the other person. Focus on *their* hurt feelings. Think about what you could say or do that would make them feel better.

- Don't spend a lot of time trying to convince the other person that you didn't mean to harm them, because they still feel hurt.

- If you need help talking to the person about what happened, ask an adult for help.

- In this story, Alex waves at the person he hurt as a way to start a conversation. Sometimes even a small gesture like a smile or a wave sends a message that you care.

WHAT TO DO IF YOU ARE THE PERSON WHO WAS HURT:
Conflict happens. When conflict takes place, both people can help to make things better. As explained above, the person who caused the harm can reach out and find a way to make it right. The person who has been hurt can be open to hearing what the person who is trying to make it better has to say. Both sides take bravery.

- Try to remember what it felt like when someone forgave you for something.

- When the person who hurt you reaches out to you, be open and listen to what they have to say.

FOR ADULTS
After Alex ruins the boy's drawing, many of the other children in the schoolyard also become upset. They start to ignore, exclude, and be mean to Alex. That kind of group dynamic can lead to more conflicts. That's why it is a good idea to talk about and work to resolve the conflict.

THESE WORDS MAY BE HELPFUL WHEN TALKING ABOUT THIS BOOK WITH CHILDREN:
Brave: Doing something you would not normally do that may be hard physically or emotionally

Conflict: A disagreement, fight, or problem

Forgive: Stop feeling angry at or hurt by a person

Impact: Have a strong effect on someone or something

Intent: What someone plans to do

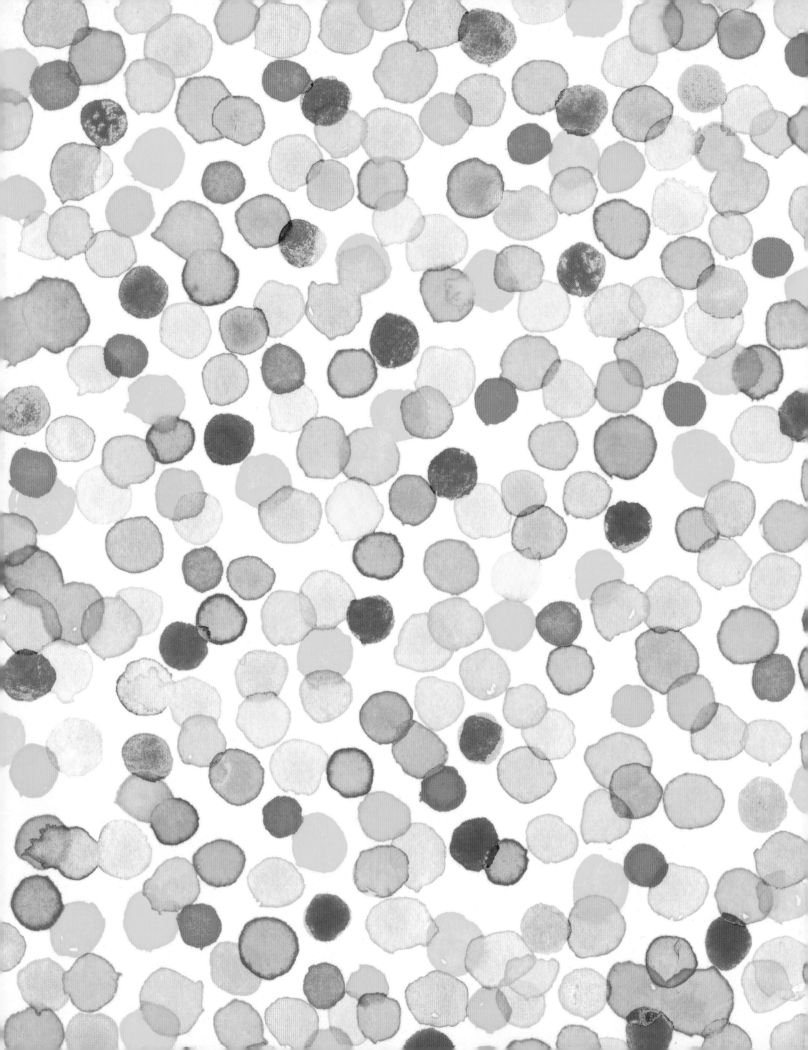